D0970433

Stories and rhymes in this book

Published by Ladybird Books Ltd
27 Wrights Lane London W8 5TZ
A Penguin Company

Produced for Ladybird Books Ltd by Nicola Baxter and Amanda Hawkes

The Fidgety Frogs

by Mandy Ross
illustrated by Carey Bennett

WHATEVER THE WEATHER

We like it
when it's
cool.

We like it when it's hot.

We like it when it's stormy.
We like it when it's not.

We like it
when it's
windy.

We like it
when it's
foggy.

But rainy weather's best because...

Our Boggy Pond gets soggy.

That's good for a froggy!

HOW THE FIDGETY FROGS BEGAN

The Fidgety Frog family lived in Boggy Pond.

There were...

Father Frog, Mother Frog

and five small Fidgety Frogs,

Freddie,

Fernando,

Fiona,

Fenella

and Frank.

One night Fenella Frog couldn't sleep for fidgeting.

When Father Frog looked in, she said, “Tell me a story, Father. Tell me how I began.”

"Well," said Father Frog, "you weren't always a Fidgety Frog.

Once you were just a tiny blob called frogspawn."

"Did I fidget then?" asked Fenella.

"No," said Father Frog,
"but then you grew a tail."

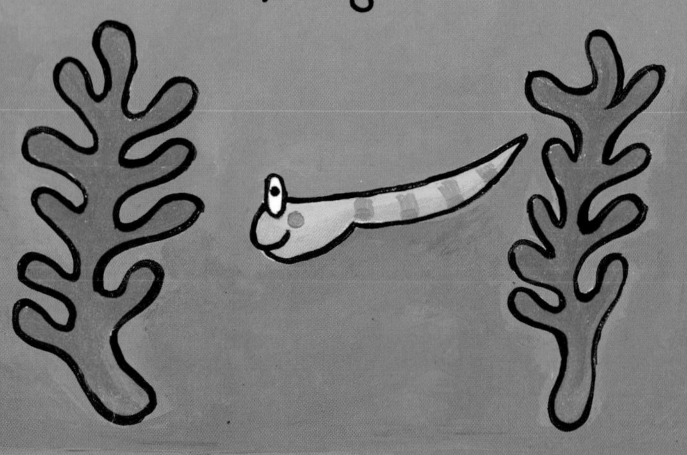

"Tell me the tale," said Fenella.

"Well, then you were a tadpole!

First you
grew your
back legs,

and then
your front
legs,

and then just last week, you
lost your tail, didn't you?"

"That was because I was fidgeting," said Fenella, fidgeting some more.

"Quite right," said Father Frog. "And now you're a fully fidgeting Fidgety Frog.

And we're all very proud of you!"
FENELLA IS FAB

READING MATTER

"I've reddit,
reddit, reddit,"
Croaked a
frog one
sunny day.

"I've read
this...

and this!

And these...
and this...
I need a NEW storybook today."

THE SITTING STILL COMPETITION

One morning, Freddie Frog
sat thinking
on a large
lily leaf.

"Let's have a Sitting
Still Competition," he said.

Fernando, Fiona,

Fenella and Frank

hopped about with excitement.

"SIT STILL!" shouted Freddie. "Let's start now."

So they did. Everything was very quiet and still.

And then...
bzzzz...
gulp!

Fernando
swallowed
a fly.

And then...
splish!
Fiona leapt
off after a
dragonfly.

And then...
swoosh!
Fenella dived underwater
to follow a fish.
And then...
splat!
Frank did
a bellyflop,
just for fun.

Which left
Freddie
sitting still
on the
lily leaf.

And then...

SPLOSH!
The Sitting Still
Competition was over!

SWISH
SWOOSH!

Wiggly little
fingers...

And wiggly
webbed toes...

Are best for swimming,
As any frog knows!

THE RAINY DAY

It was a rainy day on Boggy Pond.

Fiona Frog sat on a lily leaf, twirling a pink umbrella.

“Why do you want an umbrella?” asked the fish.

“Frogs are waterproof, aren’t they?”

But Fiona just twirled her umbrella.

And then
along came
Freddie,
Fernando,
Fenella
and Frank...
and each of them
had an umbrella, too.

"Roll up!
Roll up!"
called Fiona.
"It's time for
the show!"

Then the five small
Fidgety Frogs performed
the Twirly Umbrella Dance
on the banks of Boggy Pond.

And you should have heard the cheering from the ducks and the bees and the fish!

HAVE YOU HEARD?

"Have you heard of the Frog Prince?" a froggy asked a sweet froggess.

"If you were a Frog Prince," she said,

"I would be a Frog Princess."

FERNANDO TRIES TO FLY

"I feel like doing something new," said Fernando Frog one day.

"I think I'll try to fly."

Fernando's friend, Debbie Dragonfly, showed him how she flapped her pretty wings.
"But frogs don't have wings," said Fernando.

"You could try leaping off a rock instead," said Debbie.

"Good idea," Fernando said. He was just ready to leap...

when up
popped his
brother,
Frank.

"LOOK OUT! I'm trying to fly!" shouted Fernando, and he hopped right over Frank and landed...

in the pond.

"That was fun," laughed Frank. "Can I try?"
So Fernando sat on the rock, and...
Frank leapt right over him... SPLOSH!

Fernando Frog never did learn to fly...

but he did invent a great new game – LEAPFROG!

FROGGY LULLABY

When Boggy Pond
grows quiet,
And the moon and stars
are bright,

We croak our
froggy lullaby,
In the pale
moonlight.